I Love You More Than...

Marcy Kelman

bookoli

Gareth Llewhellin

D1635665

"Just **how much** do you love me?"

Little Tiger sighed.

"I love you more than anything!" Mama replied.

"Do you love me more than a **mouse loves cheese?**"

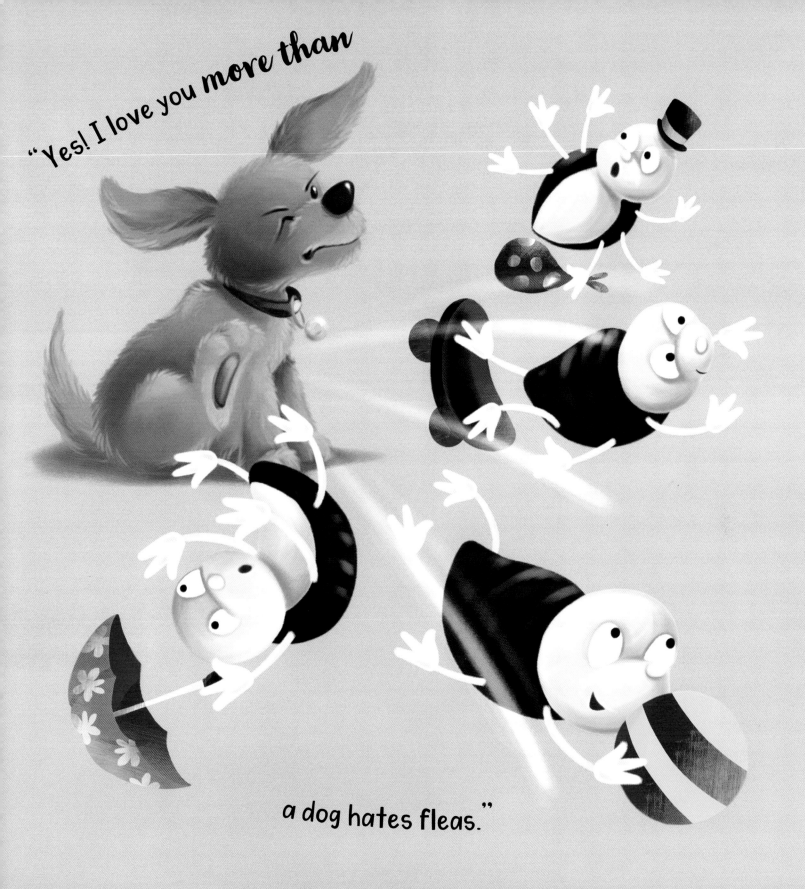

"Yes! I love you more than

a dog hates fleas."

"Do you love me more than **bears love honey**?"

"Yes! I love you **more than** a chocolate bunny."

"Do you love me more than splashing down a slide?"

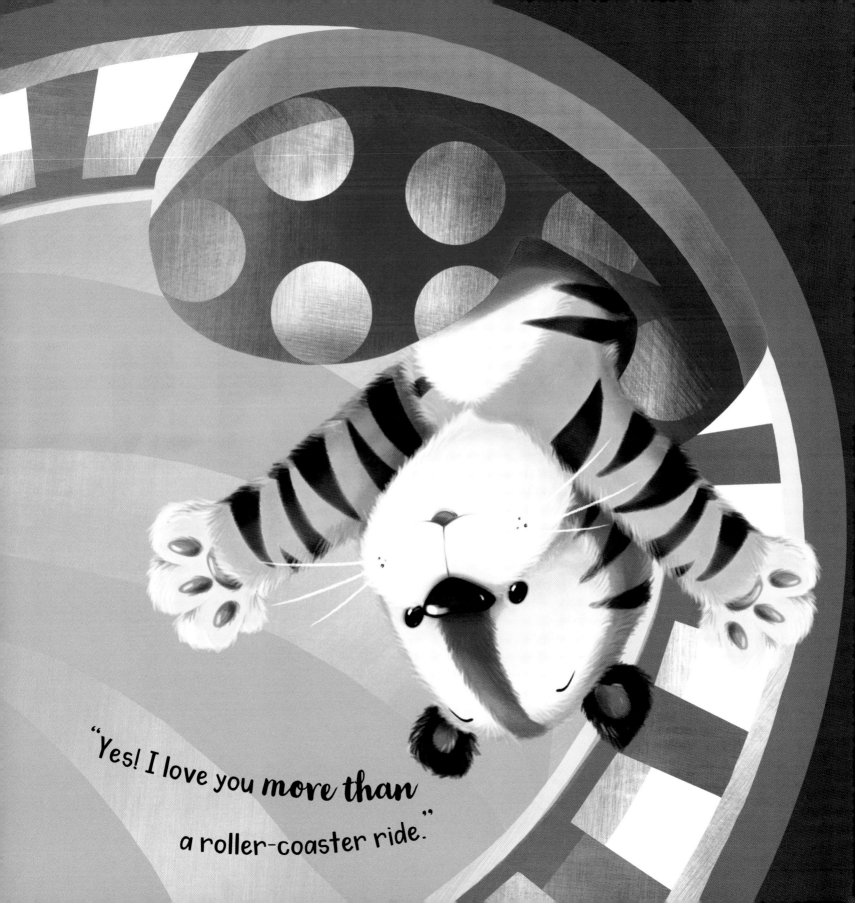

"Yes! I love you **more than** a roller-coaster ride."

"Do you love me more than a pirate loves his ship?"

"Do you love me more than *polar bears* love the cold?"

"Yes! I love you **more than** leprechauns love gold."

"Do you love me more than lions like to roar?"

"Yes! I love you *more than* dancing across the floor."

Little Tiger thought for a while, then broke into a happy smile.

"If you love me **more than** shooting down a slide,

More than racing on a

roller-coaster ride ...

"... if you love me **more than** pirates love their ships,

And **more than** doing pancake flips ...

"... well, wow! That's a lot!" Little Tiger said with a giggle.

Mama gave him a tickle,

which made Tiger **wiggle!**

"I'll always **cheer the loudest** at everything you do.

And anything you try,

I'll **always** help you through."

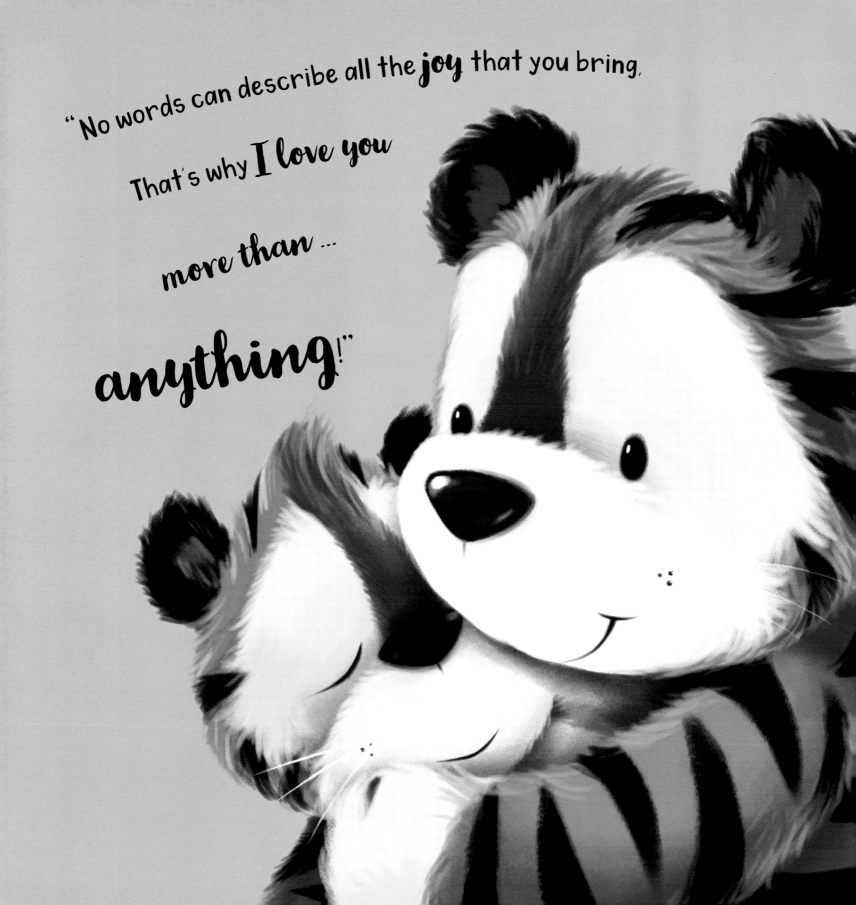

"No words can describe all the **joy** that you bring,

That's why **I** love **you**

more than ...

anything!"